TRANSFORMERS PRIME

Little, Brown and Company

Hachette Book Group
237 Park Avenue, New York, NY 10017
Visit our website at www.lb-kids.com

Little, Brown and Company is a division of Hachette Book Group, Inc.
The Little, Brown name and logo are trademarks of Hachette Book Group, Inc.

The publisher is not responsible for websites (or their content)
that are not owned by the publisher.

First Edition: September 2012

ISBN 978-0-316-18868-5

10 9 8 7 6 5 4 3 2 1

IM

Printed in China

LICENSED BY:

AUTOBOTS VERSUS ZOMBIES

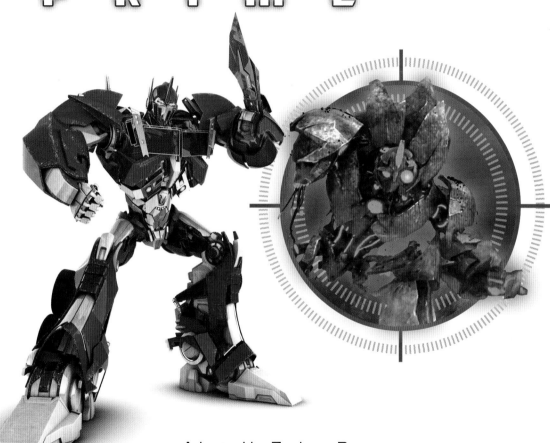

Adapted by Zachary Rau

Based on the pilot written by Duane Capizzi

LITTLE, BROWN AND COMPANY

New York Boston

Deep inside the top secret Autobot base on Earth, the Transformer named Ratchet is busy working when he is distracted by a strange sound. *CLANG!*

"Who's there?" Ratchet asks, looking around. But no one is there.

Suddenly, a piece of broken equipment mysteriously comes to life and attacks Ratchet!

"Stay still!" Ratchet yells as he swats at it. Because it is so small, the bot easily dodges Ratchet's blows.

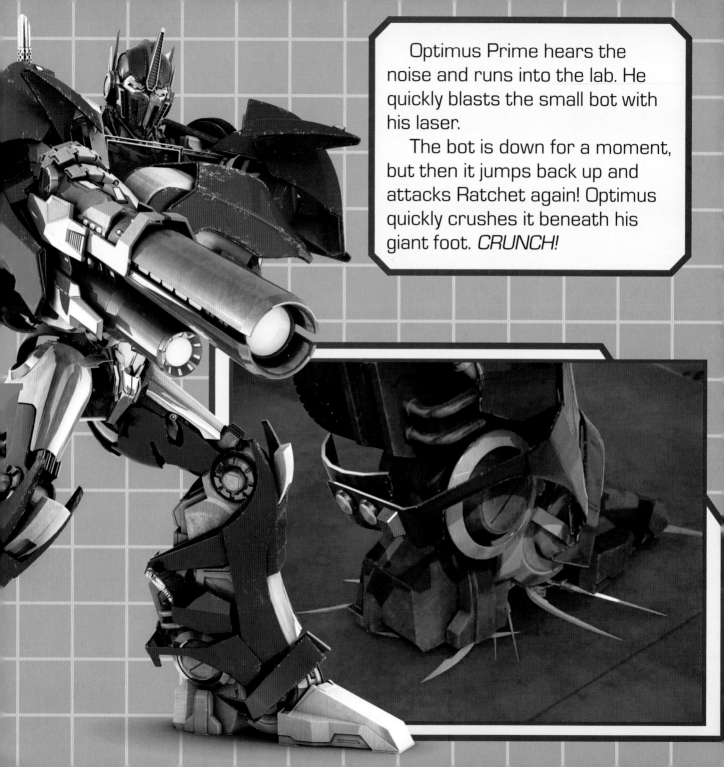

Optimus Prime hears the noise and runs into the lab. He quickly blasts the small bot with his laser.

The bot is down for a moment, but then it jumps back up and attacks Ratchet again! Optimus quickly crushes it beneath his giant foot. *CRUNCH!*

Ratchet can't believe what just happened. "What could have caused it to act that way?" he asks.

"I have a grave suspicion that it was Dark Energon," replies Optimus. "Only Dark Energon could have brought something back to life like that. I believe Megatron wants to conquer Earth with an army of zombie Transformers!"

"Where in this world would Megatron find enough robots to make an army of the undead?" asks Ratchet.

"Unfortunately, I know exactly where," replies Optimus. "We must leave right away."

Ratchet and Optimus travel in silence for many miles. They finally reach a lifeless valley filled with rocks and dirt.

"What do we hope to find here?" whispers Ratchet.

"This is the site of the largest battle between Autobots and Decepticons in this galaxy," explains Optimus. "Many perished in this fight long, long ago."

Ratchet can see there are fallen bots strewn everywhere. He confesses, "For the first time in my life, Optimus, I hoped you were wrong about something."

Suddenly, a jet streaks across the sky and lands on a rock near Optimus and Ratchet. The jet changes into a Decepticon, confirming the Autobots' worst fear: Megatron is back!

"Optimus, have you been well?" quips Megatron. "I see you brought your trusty watchdog."

"I know why you're here, Megatron," replies Optimus Prime.

"Hardly a surprise, Optimus. After all, you and I have been at this a long time," says Megatron. He tosses a large piece of Dark Energon into the valley below. "Now *your* time has come to an end!"

Energy ripples through the ground, and the forms of the ancient Transformers begin to glow.

"Rise, my army of Terrorcons!" cries Megatron. "Rise!"

The dead robots slowly come back to life, seething with the evil power of Dark Energon.

"By the AllSpark," gasps Ratchet as hundreds of ancient Transformers rise up from the dead.

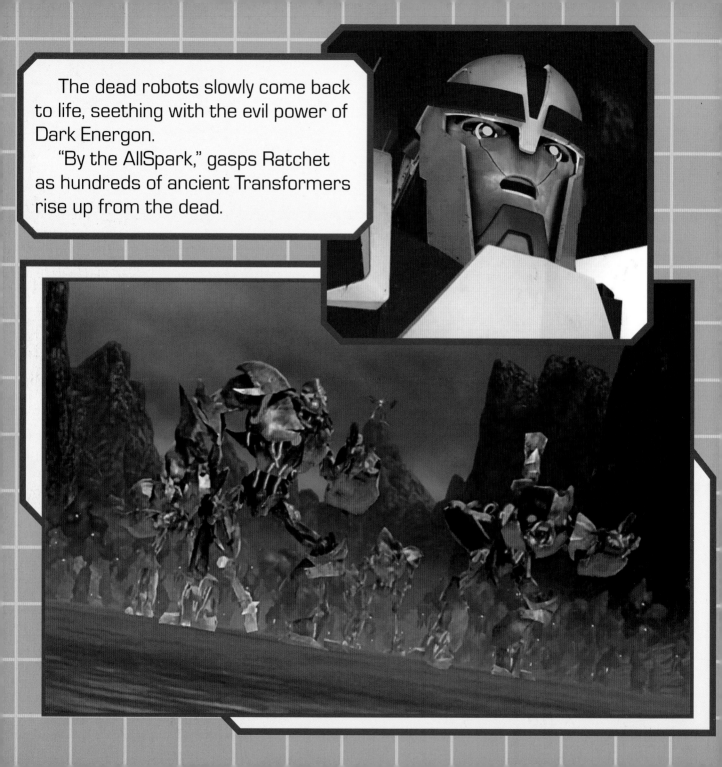

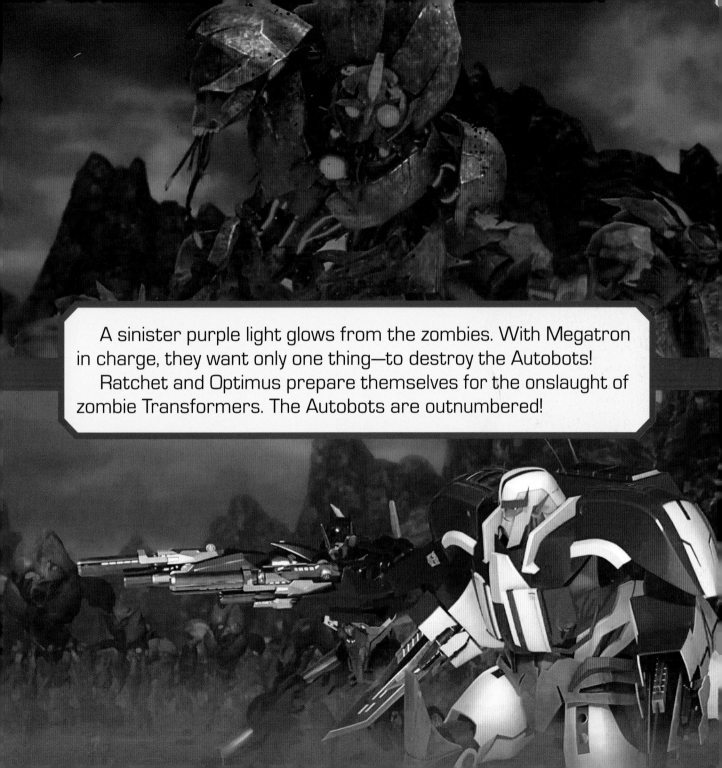

A sinister purple light glows from the zombies. With Megatron in charge, they want only one thing—to destroy the Autobots! Ratchet and Optimus prepare themselves for the onslaught of zombie Transformers. The Autobots are outnumbered!

"I have mastered Dark Energon and possess complete control over my army," Megatron taunts the Autobots with a laugh. "Destroy them!" he yells to the zombies.

Optimus quickly changes his hands into ion blasters and begins firing.

Meanwhile, Ratchet switches his hands into long blades. He slices through the herd of Terrorcons. But even as Optimus and Ratchet defeat each zombie, the scattered bots keep coming back to life!

"How can we stop them if they're already dead?" asks Ratchet.

"We must keep hope," replies Optimus.

Ratchet gets an idea. He remembers that Optimus stepped on the bot back at their base—that's how they can crush the zombies!

"I recommend breaking them into small pieces," he says to Optimus. "The smaller the better."

The plan works—but Megatron continues sending more and more of the undead into the fray. The Autobots are still greatly outnumbered.

Soon, the exposure to Dark Energon starts to affect Optimus Prime. He feels weak. The zombies jump on top of him from all directions and bury him under a pile of Terrorcons.

"Optimus?" screams Ratchet.

"We cannot falter now, Ratchet," cries Optimus Prime. He draws on the last of his energy reserves and throws off his attackers. He will not allow the Autobots to be defeated.

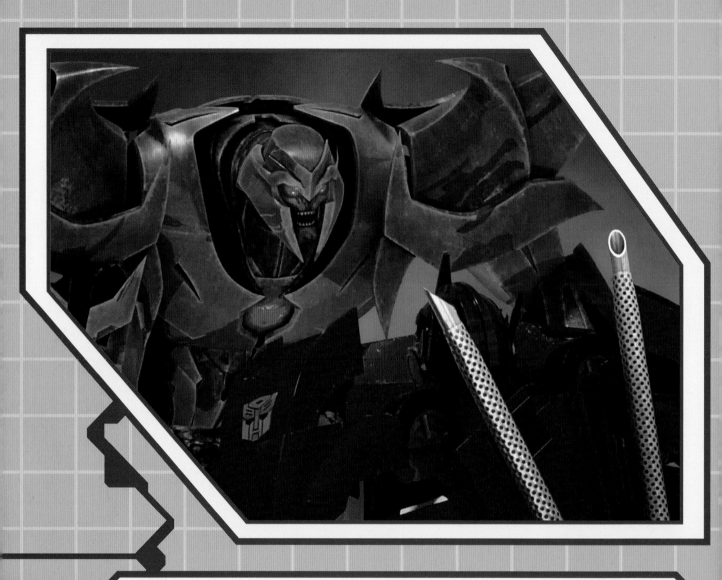

Optimus Prime climbs up onto the rock to confront Megatron himself.

"Bravo, Optimus," says Megatron, "but this is just the beginning. You may wish to save your strength for the main event."

"You will not prevail, Megatron," warns Optimus Prime. "Not while Energon still flows through my veins!"

"Fitting, for it is *Dark* Energon that flows through mine," replies Megatron. The villain changes into jet form and takes off as Optimus blasts at him. The Decepticon gets away.

Without Megatron there to control them, the Terrorcons fall to the ground, once again lifeless. The fight is over.

Ratchet joins Optimus on top of the rock. "If not to defeat us today, what is Megatron's plan for his undead army?" asks Ratchet.

"I'm afraid to ask," replies Optimus. "But if I know Megatron, whatever comes next will be much worse."